THE GIANT BOOK
MAZES

EDITED BY JEFFREY A. O'HARE

BOYDS MILLS PRESS

Published by Bell Books
Boyds Mills Press, Inc.
A Highlights Company
815 Church Street
Honesdale, Pennsylvania 18431
Printed in Mexico

Publisher Cataloging-in-Publication Data
The giant book of mazes / edited by Jeffrey A. O'Hare.—1st ed.
[72]p. : col.ill. ; cm.
Summary : Challenging mazes and labyrinths.
ISBN 1-56397-675-7
1. Puzzles—Juvenile literature. 2. Maze puzzles—Juvenile literature.
[1. Puzzles. 2. Maze puzzles.] I. O'Hare, Jeffrey A. II. Title.
793.7 /3—dc20   1997   AC   CIP
Library of Congress Catalog Card Number 96-80394

First edition, 1997
Book designed by Jeffrey George
The text of this book is set in 12-point New Century Schoolbook.

10 9 8 7 6 5 4

Raccoon Roll

Can you help Raleigh make it back to his hole?

Answer on page 65

Fur Whom the Bells Toll

Can you tell which rope pulls each bell?

Answer on page

Pizza Problem

Lead Delivery Dan across the lawn to the front door.

5

On the Job

Find the route that will get Larry across the construction site so that he can deliver the bucket of bolts to his boss.

Dotty

When Dotty saw that she had forgotten her lunch box, she ran off the bus. Now she has to walk to school. She's decided to take the shortcut through the woods and pick some mushrooms along the way. If you add up the mushrooms beside the correct path, you'll discover how many minutes late Dotty was when she reached school.

Answer on page 6

Bubble Trouble

Wanda wants to weach the water. Er, reach the water. Help her get to the tub by moving through the bubble openings without breaking any of the edges.

spaghetti slurp

Frankie, Frannie, Mario, and Maria are really enjoying their meal.
Can you tell who's eating from which plate?

Answer on page 6

Needles in a Haystack

Don't get stuck as you try to find the one path that will lead you through the haystack. You need to pick up all four needles and exit the haystack without retracing any part of your path.

Shoe Business

Find the fair way through this festival of footwear.
Keep at it and you won't suffer the agony of de-feat.

FINISH

START

Answer on page 6

Hedging Your Pets

Can you bring Betty out of this
garden without being bushwacked
by bushy beasts?

Back Track

Grab your backpack as you track back to camp. You start with ten points.
You can cross a blocked route, but if you do, you lose a point. What is the best score
you can come up with when going from START to CAMP?

Answer on page 66

Horrible Harry

Help Harry haunt the whole house by taking him from the basement to the attic and out the chimney.

Answer on page

Pieces of Eight

Pack Rat

Pat Packrat needs to collect all the shiny objects on his way home. Be careful not to bump into the Bobcat Boys.

Answer on page

Film Show

Help the projectionist thread the film so he can start the show.

Gail's Greenhouse

Gail is setting up her new greenhouse, and she's made a list of all the things she needs. Can you help Gail gather her items in the order they are listed? Watch out for bugs and don't retrace any steps.

1. Fuchsia plant
2. Seeds
3. Clay pots
4. Soil mix
5. Can for watering
6. Plant food
7. Tools
8. Plant cuttings
9. Geranium plants
10. Tuber, bulbs, rhizome
11. Christmas cactus

nswer on page 67

Goofy Gutters

Roll the drop of water through the gutters to the bucket below.

Answer on page 6

Top Banana

Oh no! A big gorilla is at large in the Big Apple.
Can you help Kong climb to the big banana
atop the Entire Fruit Building?

START→

answer on page 67

Mush Match

Follow the ropes to match each dog with the proper sled.

Answer on page 6

Donut Go This Way

It's time to make a path through the donuts.

START

FINISH

Tunnel Teaser

Which chipmunk's tunnel to the buried nut is shorter?

Answer on page 67

Hammer Time

Help John Henry, the steel-driving man, track down the golden spike.

King Crab

[F]ind a pathway to [th]e sand crab who [li]ves in this castle.

START

FINISH

[A]nswer on page 68

[A]nswer on page 67

Islands

Head to the ice-cream store
for your just desserts.

ICE CREAM

TODAY
HEAD
HUNTER
SPECIAL
COOKIES
-N-
SCREAM

Answer on page 6

Mountain Climber

Scale to new heights as you climb these cascades.

In a Cavern In a Canyon

Only the hardiest adventurers have been in these caves and found their way to the treasure. Ar
you up to the challenge? Collect as many keys as possible along the way, because each key open
a treasure chest. But beware! Each time your path is blocked by a monster or trap, you must
surrender a key to continue. Without doubling back or crossing over your path, can you find th
way that will leave you with the most keys when you arrive at the treasure?

nswer on page 68

Perplexing Pelican

Start at the pelican, scoop up all the fish and exit the maze without retracing any path.

Answer on page 6

Volcano

Help the explorers find a path across this dangerous volcano.

Star Track

Lead the starship into its home base.

Capital Idea

Go from Start to Finish by visiting only those cities that are state capitals.

Answer on page 69

A Three-Pipe Problem

Can you tell which tap leads to the problem pipe?

Frog Hop

Each frog wants to reach a lilypad of its own, without crossing the
path of any other jumper or retracing its own path.

Answer on page 69

⊔m and Becky

Guide Tom and Becky out of this underground cavern.

Home Run

Make a home run by racing through these baseballs to touch first base, second and third before ending back at home plate. Be careful. If you cross over your own path, you're out!

38

Answer on page 6.

Shell Game

Hop on board Titus's shell and find a way to reach his head.

Answer on page 69

Something's Fishy

Match each fish on the left with its duplicate on the right.
No lines may cross or go along the same corridor.

Answer on page 7

Home Time

Can you get from Jill's house to home? You need to stop off at each of your friend's houses along the way, but can't cross or backtrack along your own path.

START

Road Rally

Which racer will wind up at the finish line?

FINISH

Fish Follies

There are actually two mazes here. The fish needs to reach the pool at the bottom, while the salamander wants to get to the top of the rocks. Can you help them?

Answer on page

Asteroids

START

FINISH

Help the Pan-Galactic Conquistadors find a safe path through these asteroids.

Which Way Wonderland?

Alice wants to shuffle on home, but the cards are stacked against her.
If you help her find a path to Humpty Dumpty, she'll think you're "aces."

Answer on page 70

Pretzel Pull

Which pretzel path leads from the machine to Chef Peter?

Answer on page 7

Out In Left Field

Bubba's befuddled. He has no idea who left this strange design in his field, and he has no idea how to get from the start circle to the finish circle. Can you show him the way?

All In a Knight's Work

Lead Lancelot to the lovely lady.

Answer on page 71

All Square

Take the watering can to the flowers. You can only move on the squares, and you can only move across or up and down, but not diagonally.

Sand Span

Quick! Work your way through this maze before the tide comes in.

ENTER

EXIT

Answer on page 7

A Clockwork Challenge

Hickory, dickory dock, there's cheese atop this clock.
The mouse wants to sup, so help him run up,
Or the cheese will turn hard as a rock.

START

Answer on page 71

The Game Is A-Foot

Criminals are loose in London. Sherlock Holmes needs to travel from Big Ben to Baker Street. On the way, help him capture the three crooks who have been causing all the trouble. Don't get caught crossing back over your path or the crooks will escape.

Zig Zag Ziggurat

The golden idol awaits anyone who can climb this ancient pyramid.

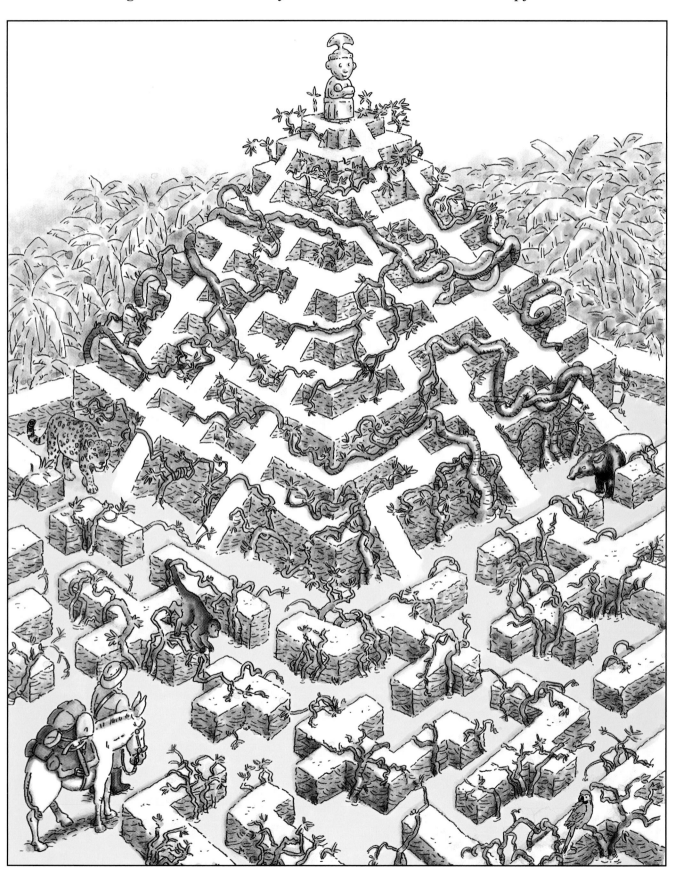

Answer on page 7

Animals of Africa

Enter the maze from here, pass through as many animals as you can, and then return here without retracing your path.

Door To Door

Which of the four paths leads to the open door?

Answer on page 7

Vine Time

Find the vine that will let Tarzan climb to his house.

1 2 3 4

Answer on page

Dangerous Dragon

Grab hold of this dragon and find the path that leads from claw to tail.

Sea Hunt

You'll have a whale of a time if you can swim your way to the sunken treasure.
Be careful or the octopus may grab you!

Answer on page 7

Maze of the Minotaur

Theseus and the Minotaur would like to get something to eat. However, before they
can go, they must rescue all the other people who are also trapped in this maze.
The trick is they must not cross their own path or double back down any hallway.
Can you find the one path they need to rescue all eight people
and reach the opening?

Runaway Rovers

Darryl was walking his dogs when they all broke loose at once.
Find the path through these dogs so Darryl can reach the bone before the dogs.

Answer on page 72

Answers

Page 3 Raccoon Roll

Page 4 For Whom the Bells Toll
1-D 2-C 3-A 4-B

Page 5 Pizza Problem

Page 6 On the Job

Page 8 Dotty
Dotty was 45 minutes late.

Page 9 Bubble Trouble

Page 10 Spaghetti Slurp
1-B 2-C 3-D 4-A

Page 11 Needles in a Haystack

Page 12 Shoe Business

Page 13 Hedging Your Pets

Page 14 Back Track

Page 16 Horrible Harry

Page 17 Pieces of Eight

F has the most gold coins.

Page 18 Pack Rat

Page 19 Film Show

Page 20 Gail's Greenhouse

Page 22 Goofy Gutters

Page 23 Top Banana

Page 24 Mush Match

Orange-3	Gray-2
Black-5	Yellow-4
Brown-1	Spotted-6

Page 25 Donut Go This Way

Page 26 Tunnel Teaser

Page 26 Hammer Time

Page 27 King Crab

Page 30 In a Cavern In a Canyon

Page 32 Perplexing Pelican

Page 28 Islands

Page 33 Volcano

Page 29 Mountain Climber

Page 33 Star Track

Page 34 Capital Idea

Page 35 A Three-Pipe Problem

Page 36 Frog Hop

Page 37 Tom and Becky

Page 38 Home Run

Page 39 Shell Game

Page 40 Something's Fishy

Page 44 Fish Follies

Page 41 Home Time

Page 45 Asteroids

Page 42 Road Rally

Page 46 Which Way Wonderland?

70

Page 48 Pretzel Pull

Page 49 Out In Left Field

Page 50 All In a Knight's Work

Page 51 All Square

Page 52 Sand Span

Page 53 A Clockwork Challenge